NUMBER THE STARS

Grades 4-6

About This Book

This well-written and fast-paced story follows the struggle by the Danish family of Annemarie Johansen to help their Jewish neighbours reach safety during the Second World War. The unit contains activities to challenge students' vocabulary, comprehension, sketching, creative writing and oral reading skills. Answer key included.

Written by: Joan Jamieson
Illustrated by: Ric Ward
Item #N1-244

Original Publication: 2000

Look For

Other Junior - Novel Studies

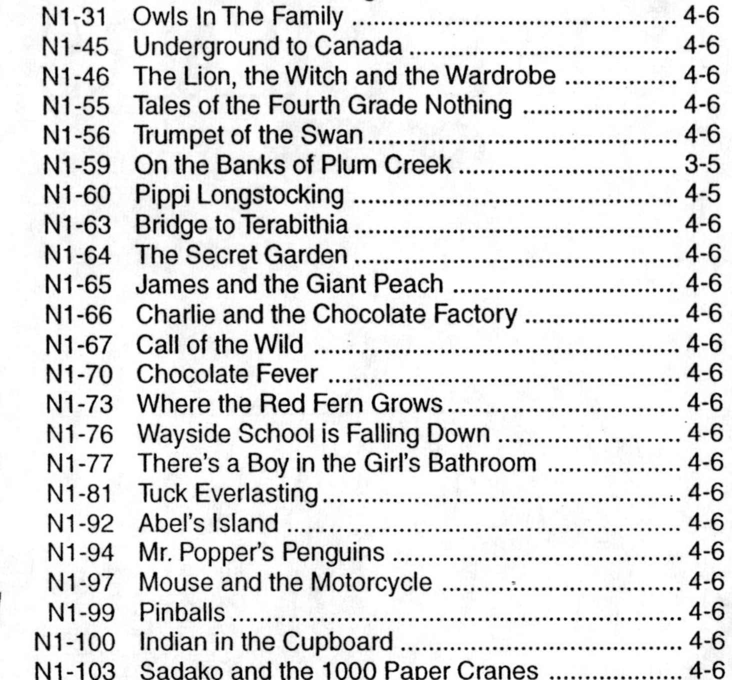

Item #	Title	Grade
N1-23	Charlotte's Web	4-6
N1-28	Little House in the Big Woods	4-6
N1-31	Owls In The Family	4-6
N1-45	Underground to Canada	4-6
N1-46	The Lion, the Witch and the Wardrobe	4-6
N1-55	Tales of the Fourth Grade Nothing	4-6
N1-56	Trumpet of the Swan	4-6
N1-59	On the Banks of Plum Creek	3-5
N1-60	Pippi Longstocking	4-5
N1-63	Bridge to Terabithia	4-6
N1-64	The Secret Garden	4-6
N1-65	James and the Giant Peach	4-6
N1-66	Charlie and the Chocolate Factory	4-6
N1-67	Call of the Wild	4-6
N1-70	Chocolate Fever	4-6
N1-73	Where the Red Fern Grows	4-6
N1-76	Wayside School is Falling Down	4-6
N1-77	There's a Boy in the Girl's Bathroom	4-6
N1-81	Tuck Everlasting	4-6
N1-92	Abel's Island	4-6
N1-94	Mr. Popper's Penguins	4-6
N1-97	Mouse and the Motorcycle	4-6
N1-99	Pinballs	4-6
N1-100	Indian in the Cupboard	4-6
N1-103	Sadako and the 1000 Paper Cranes	4-6
N1-110	Return of the Indian	4-6
N1-114	Best Christmas Pageant Ever	4-6
N1-123	Harriet the Spy	4-6
N1-133	How to Eat Fried Worms	4-6
N1-136	Hatchet	6-8
N1-139	Stone Fox	4-6
N1-154	Castle in the Attic	4-6
N1-158	Shiloh	4-6
N1-159	Summer of the Swans	4-6
N1-160	Maniac Magee	4-6
N1-176	King of the Wind	4-6
N1-178	Dear Mr. Henshaw	4-5
N1-180	Midnight Fox	4-6
N1-185	BFG	4-6
N1-187	The Whipping Boy	4-6
N1-188	A Taste of Blackberries	4-6
N1-199	Family Under the Bridge	4-6
N1-204	Bunnicula	4-6
N1-206	The War with Grandpa	4-6
N1-207	Radio Fifth Grade	4-7
N1-216	Sign of the Beaver	4-6
N1-217	Railroader	5-7
N1-223	Big Red	4-6
N1-232	Enormous Egg	4-6
N1-233	Little House on the Prairie	4-6
N1-241	Chocolate Touch	4-6
N1-243	Midwife's Apprentice	4-6
N1-244	Number the Stars	4-6
N1-245	Sounder	4-6
N1-246	Rascal	5-7

Published by:
S&S Learning Materials
15 Dairy Avenue
Napanee, Ontario
K7R 1M4

Distributed in U.S.A. by:
T4T Learning Materials
5 Columba Drive, Suite 175
Niagara Falls, New York
14305

Table of Contents

Written by Joan Jamieson

Illustrated by Ric Ward

ISBN 1-55035-664-X

Expectations

The students will:
- develop a love of and an appreciation for good literature.
- improve and extend independent reading skills.
- practise responding to literature in a variety of creative ways.
- become familiar with the problems the Jewish people had during World War II.

Summary of the Story

Number The Stars

Annemarie Johansen is a ten year old girl who lives with her family in Copenhagen. The Nazis have been occupying Denmark for three years, and Annemarie and her friend Ellen have become quite accustomed to seeing soldiers on every corner. Little sister Kirsti isn't even afraid of them as she cannot remember a time when there were no soldiers.

Annemarie has already suffered tragedy in her life. Three years ago in a traffic accident her beloved eighteen year old sister Lise was killed. Annemarie often peeks into the blue trunk to admire Lise's trousseau, particularly the wedding dress in which she was to have been married just two weeks after her death. Her fiancé Peter Nielson still comes around to visit the younger girls and talk to their parents, but things are just not the same any more.

When the Nazis demand the list of Danish Jews from the rabbis in the synagogue, the underground Resistance movement swings into action and the citizens of Denmark are called upon to hide their Jewish friends and neighbours. Dark-haired Ellen is sent to the Johansen family for shelter, and at this point the tension begins to mount.

Annemarie and Ellen are asleep when Nazi soldiers come looking for Ellen's family, the Rosens. It's difficult for the Johansens to pass off dark haired Ellen as a member of their family, but quick thinking on Mr. Rosen's part saves them all. A trip to the country where Jewish citizens are being smuggled to Sweden continues to raise the level of suspense and carries the novel to its conclusion.

The story of how the Danish people helped their Jewish neighbours to safety consumes the rest of the book. Annemarie and Ellen are called upon to grow up quickly into an understanding far beyond their years. The day to day heroism of Danish citizens in the face of adversity is celebrated at a level in which young people can easily participate.

This story is extremely well written and moves along quickly. It's a wonderful book to read aloud to a class, or for students to read on their own. It provides a wealth of opportunity to explore the historical fiction aspects of its setting. As well as details of the Second World War, the story brings alive many concepts of life during a war such as rationing and the need for blackouts. An afterward by the author provides interesting details about where the historical reality leaves off and fiction begins.

Author Biography

Lois Lowry

Lois Lowry was born in 1937, in Hawaii. Her family separated soon after her birth, and she moved with her mother to the Amish area of Pennsylvania. Lois was much adored by her maternal grandfather who protected her from the horrors of the Second World War.

As an author, Ms. Lowry concentrates on a variety of themes concerning young people and the difficulties they face in their lives. She stated that she measures her own success as a novelist through her ability to "help adolescents answer their own questions about life, identity, and human relationships."

In her first novel, A Summer to Die, the Chalmers family move to the country for the summer where teenagers Meg and Molly share a room. A series of nosebleeds draw everyone's attention to Molly, the 15-year-old sister. As Molly becomes sicker, 13-year-old younger sister Meg realizes that her sibling is slowly dying from leukemia. Meg turns for friendship and support to Will Banks, a neighbour who encourages her burgeoning interest in photography. Ben and Maria involve Meg, through her pictures, in the birth of their child.

This book was well received by critics who felt that it dealt with a difficult topic with sensitivity and a sense of completion without manipulating the readers' emotions. Lowry's interest in the story of Meg and Molly was drawn from her own life: her older sister Helen died of cancer when Lois was a young woman.

In future novels, Lowry continued to focus on the challenges young people face in growing up. Her next book, "Find a Stranger, Say Goodbye", deals with an adopted daughter's search for her biological mother. Although this topic does not stem from anything in her personal life, Lowry felt it was important enough in the lives of others to make it the theme for her novel.

Lowry's most popular character began to appear in her novels in 1979. Anastasia Krupnik is a ten-year-old hero who faces a series of comic crises in a series of books. Ms. Lowry reports that "Until I was about twelve I thought my parents were terrific, wise, wonderful, beautiful, loving and well-dressed. By age twelve and a half they had turned into stupid boring people with whom I did not want to be seen in public." This common

phenomena repeats itself throughout many of the Anastasia stories. As each crisis hits, the young girl learns more about herself, and by the end of the book is ready to move on to a higher level of maturity. "Anastasia Krupnik", "Anastasia Again", and "Anastasia at Your Service" mark the beginnings of this ongoing series.

In "Rabble Starkey", Lowry returns to a more serious tone. The hero of this story is twelve year old Parable Ann, aka "Rabble" who was born when her mother was fourteen. She now lives with her mom and the Bigelow family. Mrs. Bigelow is hospitalized for mental illness, and the care of her infant son falls to Rabble and her young friend Veronica Bigelow. This book was well received and garnered a Child Study Award in 1987.

"Number the Stars", published in 1989, earned Lowry the Newbery medal, her highest honour yet. Set against the backdrop of Nazi-occupied Denmark during the Second World War, the story focuses on ten year old Annemarie Johansen and her family as they help the Danish Resistance movement to shelter Danish Jews.

Lowry continues to write novels for adolescents that reflect a variety of emotional experiences without sacrificing the thrill of a good story.

Books by the Lois Lowry

A Summer to Die, Houghton, 1977.
Find a Stranger, Say Goodbye, Houghton, 1978.
Anastasia Krupnik, Houghton, 1979.
Autumn Street, Houghton, 1979.
Anastasia Again!, Houghton, 1981.
Anastasia at Your Service, Houghton, 1982.
Taking Care of Terrific, Houghton, 1983.
Anastasia Ask Your Analyst, Houghton, 1984.
Us and Uncle Fraud, Houghton, 1984.
One Hundredth Thing About Caroline, Houghton, 1985.
Anastasia on Her Own, Houghton, 1985.
Switcharound, Houghton, 1985.
Anastasia has the Answers, Houghton, 1985.
Rabble Starkey, Houghton, 1987.
Anastasia's Chosen Career, Houghton, 1987.
All About Sam, Houghton, 1988.
Number the Stars, Houghton, 1989.
Your Move, J.P.!, Houghton, 1990.
Anastasia at This Address, Houghton, 1991.
Attaboy, Sam! Houghton, 1992.
The Giver, Houghton.

Student Supplies

Each student will need the following items:

1. A copy of the novel.

2. A copy of the question pages.

3. A notebook in which to record their answers. If you use the small Junior size notebooks they will fit easily into the plastic bags recommended in #7.

4. A blank sketchbook. This can easily be made by photocopying the sample page in this guide and stapling several copies together within a cover. Alternatively, sketches can be done on blank paper and glued into the students' notebook.

5. Pencil crayons. It's a good idea for each student to have their own set of pencil crayons that they keep with their novel study at all times. This ensures that they are able to complete the sketching work whether they are working in the classroom, at home, or elsewhere.

6. A large ziplock plastic bag in which to keep all of their novel study supplies. This really helps students to stay organized, and prevents leaving part of the equipment at home and part at school. And, for the benefit of the teacher, it keeps paperback novels in good enough shape to be reused over many years.

Organizing and Scheduling for Novel Studies

Grouping:

Novel studies work well as independent activities for students. If several different novels are chosen that are grouped around a theme, for example "young people coping with challenges in their lives", "novels set in another part of the world", or "historical fiction" several different novels at different levels can be studied at once. This accommodates various skill development levels and allows students to participate and grow through their experience.

Size of Groups:

Groups work best when they have five or six students in them. Fewer than that, and the level of interaction and variety of responses among the students decreases. More

than that, and some students will not feel comfortable in participating in the discussions. If you have many students reading at the same level, and are able to obtain lots of copies of one novel, you can easily have more than one group working on the same novel.

Scheduling:

If you schedule as many novel study periods per week as you have groups, you can meet with each group on a regular weekly basis to allow them time to share the work they have done with peers. During this time, students in the other groups work independently on the assignment for their next meeting, or work with another adult. (See Suggestions for Scheduling chart.)

Group Meetings:

In order to allow more frequent group meetings, try to involve teacher-librarians, special education staff, educational assistants, students teachers and volunteers to meet with the groups on occasion. This is particularly valuable for groups that require more teacher direction, or are not yet able to handle large assignments independently. A meeting outline sheet (see enclosed) for each group meeting makes this procedure viable and easy to manage, even for an adult who may not have read the novel! Students will enjoy sharing their work with another adult in a small group, and being the experts on the answers, too!

Classroom Resources:

A strong feeling for the setting is vital to the comprehension of this novel. Before beginning the novel, it is recommended that teachers gather as many resources as possible. Picture books set in Denmark, maps of the area or reference texts with lots of pictures of the clothing, housing and the geography of this area of the world will be helpful. Access to this material will make students' work on the sketching sections much more meaningful.

Types of Questions

Vocabulary:

These questions are intended to enrich and extend the students' vocabulary. They also give practise in writing concise definitions in dictionary style. Students should be encouraged, when they use words in sentences of their own, to write about a subject

that has nothing to do with the novel. They may need help at first in constructing sentences that illustrate their understanding of the word. For example, "The house is enormous," is a sentence that does use the word correctly, but does not illustrate the meaning. Used this way, enormous could mean "green" or "old" and still make sense in the sentence. "Although I was hungry, I still couldn't finish eating the enormous sundae," is a much better example of a sentence that illustrates the meaning.

Explanations and Inference:

These questions check the students' comprehension of some of the concepts in the story and their ability to infer meaning from what has been implied. The questions also provide practice in writing to explain why and how, and in expanding answers to give full explanations accompanied by supportive detail.

Sketching:

These questions check students' comprehension of the story and attention to detail. Some also provide practice drawing action within a setting. Students will learn to include as much detail as possible, and to choose their colour palettes carefully to reflect the mood of the scene. The booklet used for sketching could become a source of pride, particularly for those students who do not consider themselves to be strong in constructing written answers.

Creative Writing:

Here are many opportunities for students to create a variety of responses to what they have read. They will practise description, giving instructions, writing in role, list making, writing conversation, journal entries, letter writing, creating a script, and other forms of creative expression.

Oral Reading and Speaking:

Opportunities are provided for students to select their own passage to read, using the criteria given, and in many cases to comment upon their choice. They practise choosing a selection for a specific purpose, and finding supporting details. This section also gives them a chance to speak extemporaneously to the group on a specified topic, and to react to each others' work. Students are expected to practise their reading in advance so that when they read to the group, their presentation will be the best they have to offer.

Student/Teacher Conference Sheet

Novel Study: ______________________________

Date of Meeting: ______________________________

Teacher or Other Adult: ______________________________

Reminders From Previous Meeting:

____

____

____

____

Focus of Meeting:

____

____

____

____

____

____

Work Assigned for Next Meeting:

____

____

____

____

Date of Meeting: ______________________________

NUMBER
THE STARS
BY LOIS LOWRY
NAME:

Chapter 1: Why Are You Running?

1. For each of the words given, write a short definition that makes sense to you. You may use a dictionary if you need to, or use context to help you figure it out. Then write the word in a sentence of your own to show you understand what it means. The first one is done for you as an example. (page numbers in brackets)

a) "Go!", shouted Annemarie, and the two girls were off, racing along the **residential** sidewalk. (1)

residential - in a neighbourhood where people live
I'd rather live in the country on a farm than in a **residential** neighbourhood.

b) Three years, Annemarie thought with **contempt**. (3)

contempt - ______________________________

c) He **prodded** the corner of her backpack with the stock of his rifle. (3)

prodded - ______________________________

d) You look like **hoodlums** when you run. (5)

hoodlums - ______________________________

e) But their **uneasy** looks didn't change. (7)

uneasy - ______________________________

f) She's **exaggerating**, as she always does. (7)

exaggerate - ______

g) . . . about the news they received that way: news of **sabotage** against the Nazis . . .

sabotage - ______

2. Authors use adjectives to describe their nouns to make their language writing exact, to help paint a word picture for us. Find each of these adjectives in the text. Tell what noun it is used to describe, and what effect it creates in your mind. The first one is done for you as an example.

a) **stocky** (1)

Lois Lowry uses the word stocky to describe Annemarie. This means that she is short, and strong and muscular, not tall and skinny.

b) **lanky** (1)

______

c) **stubborn** (4)

______

d) **obstinate** (4)

______

e) **impassive** (10)

3. Do a **mini research project** to find out what you can about each of these topics. You may find some help in a dictionary, an encyclopedia, or you may have luck asking an adult, looking at the library, or checking the internet. Take some point form notes from your sources so that you will be ready to share your finding with your study group. Good luck with your research.

   a) Copenhagen
   b) the Resistance movement
   c) Denmark
   d) Die Frie Danske
   e) Nazi occupation

4. Compare your life with Annemarie's. Use a chart to do this comparison, and write in point form. Try to find at least 5 areas in which you can make a comparison. (Here are a few to get you started: travel to and from school, snacks and treats you enjoy; how you spend your free time; rules your parents have for you)

Chapter 2: Who Is the Man Who Rides Past?

1. For each of the words given, write a short definition that makes sense to you. You may use a dictionary if you need to, or use context to help you figure it out. Then, write the word in a sentence of your own to show you understand what it means.

a) "Where is his **bodyguard**?" the soldier had asked. (13)
bodyguard - ____

____

____

____

b) . . . lacy edging of a pillowcase, part of Lise's **trousseau**.(14)
trousseau - ____

____

____

____

c) . . . Lise's pillowcases with their **crocheted** edges, . . . (16)
crocheted - ____

____

____

____

d) . . . always a source of foolishness and **pranks**. (17)
pranks - ____

____

____

____

e) He seemed much older, and very tired, **defeated**. (17)
defeated - ____

____

____

____

f) Redheaded Peter, her sister's **fiancé**, had not married . . . (17)
fiancé - ____

____

____

____

2. **Proper nouns** are nouns that name a specific person, place or thing. Tell whatever details you can about each of these proper nouns that are mentioned in this chapter. Use the information given in the chapter, and add to your answer with additional research where possible.

a) Amelienborg: ______________________________

b) Hans Christian Andersen: ______________________________

c) Peter Neilson: ______________________________

d) Jubilee: ______________________________

e) Christian X: ______________________________

f) Sweden: ______________________________

g) Uncle Henrik: ______________________________

h) Norway, Holland, Belgium and France: ______________________________

i) Kattegat: ______________________________

3. Write a three paragraph character sketch of the King of Denmark. Use each paragraph to focus on one of his personality traits. Prove your statement using information from the story. Make sure your character sketch has an interesting introduction and conclusion. (One sample paragraph is done for you as an example.)

   King Christian is a very brave man. There are Nazi troops stationed on every corner in Copenhagen, and they probably would want to kill him if they knew who he was. Still, he rides his horse through the streets each day without even one bodyguard to protect him.

4. Choose one of the characters we have met so far in the story. Find a section, about one-half page in length, where you learn a lot about this character. Practise reading this selection out loud until you can do it fluently and with appropriate expression. Be prepared to read it aloud to your study group, and to explain to the members of the group just what you have learned about this character from your selection, and how you learned it.

Chapter 3: Where is Mrs. Hirsch?

1. Authors use verbs to indicate to their readers exactly what action is taking place. Find the verb on the page indicated, and explain what the author wants the reader to understand by this choice of verb. The first one is done for you as an example.

a) What did Annemarie do before she glanced at her mother? (19)

Lois Lowry says that Annemarie hesitated. She waited a bit because she was worried that her mother would be upset if she had said the wrong thing.

b) What was special about electricity? (18)

c) What had the Johansens done with their little stove? (18)

d) What did Samuel do with his eyes? (20)

e) What did Peter accuse the Nazis of doing to Jewish people? (24)

f) What did Annemarie do with her shoulders? (25)

g) What was Annemarie doing under the blanket? (26)

2. Do a **mini research project** to find out what you can about each of these topics. You may find some help in a dictionary, an encyclopedia, or you may have luck asking an adult, looking at the library, or checking the internet. Choose one of the following topics and write a one-paragraph summary about your findings.

   a) kroner
   b) swastika
   c) curfew
   d) Jews

3. In this chapter and throughout the novel, Lois Lowry uses lots of **children's stories** and games. Sometimes these are well-known fairy tales, and sometimes they are the fantasies that the girls make up.

   Draw **two illustrations**, one from the fairy tale that Annemarie told Kirsti in Chapter 2, and the other from their real life. Make the sketches as contrasting as you can using colour and lots of detail. As you share the sketches with your study group, be ready to tell us why you think the author uses these stories.

4. Choose a passage of about one-half page in length where the author evoked a strong emotion in you. Practise reading it orally so that you can convey that emotion to your listeners through your reading. Be prepared to explain to the group what feelings you had, and the specific words or phrases the author used that caused you to feel that way.

Chapter 4: It Will Be a Long Night

1. Descriptive writing uses adjectives to give the reader a mind picture of what is being described. For each noun given, find the adjective (s) used to describe it, and tell about the image created in your mind. The first one is done for you as an example.

a) **hair styles and clothes** (27)
The girls are playing with paper dolls that have old-fashioned hair styles and clothes. I see in my mind ladies with dresses and hair that remind me of the people at the Senior's home, or pictures in books my grandmother read when she was little.

b) **Ellen** (find two) - (27)

c) **Kirsti's face** (find two) - (27)

d) **Mama's look** (28)

e) **fireworks** (31)

f) **ships** (find two) - (32)

2. Authors don't tell us absolutely everything. They assume we can **infer**, or figure out what something means, by the details they have given us. Use your own words to explain what you can infer from each of these situations. The first one is done for you as an example.

a) The girls cut pictures from magazines and play with them.

I can infer that these are creative girls who like to use their imaginations. They don't get to go to real parties or wear fancy dresses any more, but they can relive happier times through their games. I can also infer that during the occupation there was probably no money to buy toys, or perhaps no toys in the stores to buy, so the girls have created their own games.

b) Ellen's father dyed Kirsti's shoes for her.

____

____

____

____

c) The Danish people blew up their own navy.

____

____

____

____

____

d) Ellen sleeps over on a school night and the girls are allowed to talk and giggle as much as they want.

____

____

____

____

____

e) The city had to be totally dark at night.

____

____

____

____

____

3. Use any resource you need to research these terms. Write one or two sentences to explain what each one means. In your short explanation, include as much detail as you can.

a) **rabbi**:

b) **synagogue**:

c) **congregation**:

d) **relocation**:

4. Work in a group of four to create a Reader's Theatre presentation of the first four pages of this chapter, ending with "she can ride on the carousel". Take the roles of Annemarie, Ellen, Kirsti and Mrs. Johansen. In Reader's Theatre, you read only the direct speech: leave parts like "she announced in a high pretend voice" out of your reading, but use them to help you gain insight into your performance. Practise your reading so that you can bring your characters to life for us.

Chapter 5: Who Is The Dark-Haired One?

1. Find a word or a phrase which is a synonym for each of these words or phrases:

a) **in a snobbish or haughty way** (39) - ______________________________

b) **spoke** (39) - ______________________________

c) **send you** (40) - ______________________________

d) **speak quietly, so you can hardly be understood** (42) - ______________________________

e) **walk, taking large steps** (44) - ______________________________

f) **looking intently** (44) - ______________________________

g) **express disagreement with something** (44) - ______________________________

h) **a disdainful look** (47) - ______________________________

i) **not flinching** (48) - ______________________________

j) **made a mark by pushing so hard** (49) - ______________________________

2. In this chapter, the tension of the story is really starting to build. Lois Lowry has chosen her words carefully to create this effect. For example, instead of just "someone said", Lowry writes "a deep voice asked the question loudly" (43). This helps us to hear the sound of the soldier's voice piercing the quiet night of their apartment. Find at least five more phrases that Lowry has written which help you to feel the tension mounting.

____

3. Use any resource you need to research these terms. Write one or two sentences to explain what each one means. In your short explanation, include as much detail as you can.

a) **Lutheran** - ____________________

b) **Star of David** - ____________________

c) **blackout curtains** - ____________________

4. Just as the Star of David has been imprinted into Annemarie's palm, so will the details of this night remain with her for a long time. When important or traumatic things happen to us, whether they are good or bad, the details stay fixed in our memories for much longer than the details of an ordinary day. We can remember exactly what we were wearing, what the weather was like, what we ate, and exactly what everyone said.

Think about a time in your life when something major happened, and about which you still have very clear memories. Write a one or two sentence introduction to your story, and one or two sentence conclusion. Make some point form notes about all rest of the details, in an order that makes sense to you. Be prepared to tell this story to your study group members, using the sentences you have written to begin and end your story, and speaking from your notes and from memory for the rest.

____

Chapter 6: Is the Weather Good For Fishing?

1. Locate the word or phrase on the page given. Explain what the word means, and tell why this was happening in the story. The first one is done for you as an example.

a) **tentatively** (50) -

Ellen and Annemarie are smiling tentatively. These would be uncertain smiles because the girls are still nervous from the soldiers' visit. They want to smile because they think it is funny to imagine Lise being bald, but they're still scared about everything that has happened, so they are being tentative.

b) **in amazement** (51) - ______________________________

c) **reluctantly** (52) - ______________________________

d) **puzzled** (52) - ______________________________

e) **heart sank** (55) - ______________________________

f) **in exasperation** (57) - ______________________________

2. Reread page 54. It might seem odd for an author to include a section where people look out of a train window and talk about the deer, when they can't actually see any deer. Think about this. Why would Lowry include this little piece of the story? Write to explain why Mama tells Ellen about the deer. (Hint: Think about who else in the story is hiding, but some day will be free.)

3. Imagine you are Ellen. How your life has turned around in the last two days! Just before you go to sleep tonight, you settle down to write your journal entry. Be sure to include details of what happened, and your feelings about it all.

Dear Diary:

4. Lois Lowry is an author who is very skilled at painting word picture in our minds. Find a paragraph or two where the picture was very clear for you, and practise reading it aloud. When you read to your study group, be prepared to tell them some specific words or phrases that helped make the picture come to life for you.

b) Draw the picture that you saw in your mind, and show it to us while you read aloud.

Chapter 7: The House By The Sea

1. For each of the words given, write a short **definition** that makes sense to you. You may use a dictionary if you need to, or use context to help you figure it out. Then, write the word in a sentence of your own to show you understand what it means. Refer to the example in chapter two to remind yourself how to do this.

a) The house and **meadows** that surrounded it were so much a part of her childhood... (60)

meadows - ______________________________

____

____

____

b) Ellen **cupped** one hand across her eyes and looked across the water . . . (62)

cupped - ______________________________

____

____

____

c) . . . looked across the water at the misty **shoreline** that was another country. (62)

shoreline - ______________________________

____

____

____

d) That's where they **unload** their fish. (62)

unload - ______________________________

____

____

____

e) . . . she outlined one of the **appliquéd** birds with her finger. (65)

appliquéd - ______________________________

____

____

____

f) In earlier times, she had always **overheard** laughter. (66)

overheard - ______________________________

____

____

____

2. Imagine you are Ellen. Just as you are telling Annemarie how much you miss your parents, the telephone rings and you are called to speak with them. Write the conversation you would have with either your mother or your father. Use script format, as though you were writing a little play.

3. Imagine that Number the Stars is being made into a movie. You have been hired as the Set Designer, which means it is your job to design and draw the sets where the actors will play their parts. You must provide enough detail that the crew can build them according to your designs. Make a sketch for one scene from this chapter using the details given in the chapter to help you label your sketches. You may need to add some close up views of certain sections so that the builders can see the details. Complete this drawing in your sketch book.

4. While you are showing your sketch to the members of your study group, read aloud the section of the chapter from which those details came. Make sure you practise your reading so that you can read from the text while pointing to the details on your drawing.

Chapter 8: There Has Been a Death

1. Find a word or a phrase which is a synonym for each of these words or phrases:

a) **mist** (67) - ______

b) **annoyed** (67) - ______

c) **make someone feel better** (68) - ______

d) **jug** (69) - ______

e) **bunch of flowers** (70) - ______

f) **loud and deep** (70) - ______

g) **sparkling** (71) - ______

h) **running lightly and quickly** (72) - ______

i) **coffin** (72) - ______

j) **someone who is grumpy** (73) - ______

k) **someone who chastises you** (73) - ______

l) **someone who bothers you in a friendly way** (73) - ______

2. Annemarie and Ellen have some extra time today, so they decide to write a letter to their friend from school back in Copenhagen. Each girl writes alternate paragraphs of the letter telling what has happened to them over the last few days. Write that letter for them, figuring out a way to show which girl wrote each paragraph.

   Dear ______________________________,

   ____
   ____
   ____
   ____
   ____
   ____
   ____
   ____
   ____
   ____
   ____
   ____
   ____
   ____
   ____
   ____
   ____
   ____
   ____
   ____

3. Imagine you are an artist who has been hired to illustrate this novel. Reread the paragraph on page 69 beginning "Kirsti joined their laughter . . . ." This paragraph emphasizes the contrast between the scene at the breakfast table, and what is going on back in Copenhagen. Your editor says you may only use one picture to show both aspects of this scene. How could you do that? Draw the picture you will submit to your editor.

4. Sometimes when you read a novel, the author paints such a lovely word picture of the setting and characters that you wish you could live right in the story. At other times, the author paints a picture equally clearly of a place you wouldn't want to be, and you are so grateful you don't live there. Choose a selection of about one half page that fulfils one of these options for you, and practise reading it aloud. When you share it with your study group, use your voice to help your listeners experience the same reaction you did.

Chapter 9: Why Are You Lying?

1. For each of the words underlined, write a short definition that makes sense to you. You may use a dictionary if you need to, or use context to help you figure it out.

a) The kitten had **fled** when she tried to dress it. . . . (74)

fled - ______________________________

b) Annemarie leaned against the ancient **splintery** wood of the barn wall . . . (74)

splintery - ______________________________

c) His strong hands continued, **deftly** pressing like a pulse against the cow. (75)

deftly - ______________________________

d) The bucket was half full, **frothy** on the top. (75)

frothy - ______________________________

e) She was **startled**. (76)

startled - ______________________________

f) . . . it is time for the night of **mourning** to begin. (77)

mourning - ______________________________

g) The **gleaming** wooden casket rested on its supports . . . (78)

gleaming - ______________________________

h) . . . surrounded by the **fragile**, papery flowers that Annemarie and Ellen had picked that afternoon. (78)

fragile - ______________________________

i) . . . Kirsti had **trudged** upstairs with her dolls under one arm and the kitten under the other. (78)

trudged - ______________________________

j) Uncle Henrik **gestured** them inside. (79)

gestured - ______________________________

k) From the living room came a sound of a baby's brief **wail**. (79)

wail - ______________________________

l) Annemarie stood in the doorway, watching the **mourners** as they sat in the candlelit room. (80)

mourners - ______________________________

m) He stared beyond the **gnarled** apple tree into the darkness. (80)

gnarled - ______________________________

n) Annemarie watched, still holding the **wedge** of firm cheese in her hand. (81)

wedge - ______________________________

o) . . . like a little girl, her bare legs **dangling** against her father's chest. (81)

dangling - ______________________________

2. Again, we will focus on the word pictures that Lois Lowry is able to paint. Read parts of this chapter again, searching for phrases that paint a clear picture for you. Find at least three examples where the picture is clear. Make a coloured sketch of each one in your sketch book, and write the phrase or sentence under it. Here is one example.

Example: (page 74)

He was kneeling on the straw-covered floor beside the cow, his shoulder pressed against her heavy side, his strong tanned hands rhythmically urging her milk into the spotless bucket.

3. Use your own words to explain what the author means in these phrases. The first one is done for you as an example.

a) . . . she knew it was better, safer, for Ellen to believe in Great-aunt Birte. (79)

Annemarie remembered what her Uncle Henrik had told her, that sometimes it is hard to lie when you know the truth, but if you don't know the truth your answers will be more believable. So, if Ellen doesn't know that there is no Great-aunt Birte in the casket, then she will not have any trouble keeping the secret.

b) In that moment, with that look, they became equals. (79)

c) It is much easier to be brave if you do not know everything. (76)

d) He smiled wryly. (77)

e) There was no playfulness in his affection tonight, just a sense of urgency, of worry. (81)

f) Why hadn't these people brought food? (80)

4. You are going to 'perform' a section of this chapter as Reader's Theatre. You will read as though you are acting the part on stage, but you will have your books to guide you, and you will remain seated throughout. Use narrative such as "he said in a low, relieved voice" to help you decide how this sentence should be read, but do not read these phrases out loud.

   You will need a partner so that one of you can be Annemarie and the other Uncle Henrik. Practise with your partner so that you can do a smooth reading for your study group. Begin on page 76 where Uncle Henrik says "I think that is not true", and end on page 77 when he says, "Are you ready?"

Chapter 10: Let Us Open the Casket

1. For each word listed, write a concise definition and then use the word in a sentence of your own to demonstrate that you understand its meaning. For an example of how to do this, refer to chapter 1.

A)

Word	Meaning
a) dozed (83)	
b) tensed (83)	
c) recurring (83)	
d) staccato (83)	
e) focusing (84)	
f) condescending (84)	
g) typhus (85)	
h) spattered (86)	
i) mantel (86)	
j) psalm (86)	

B) **Sentences**:

dozed - ______________________________

tensed - ______________________________

recurring - ______________________________

staccato - ____

focusing - ____

condescending - ____

typhus - ____

spattered - ____

mantel - ____

psalm - ____

2. In your own words, explain what the following passages mean. There is an example of how to do this in chapter 9.

a) I know it is the custom to pay one's respects by looking your loved one in the face. (85)

____

b) Of course we will open the casket. I'm glad you suggested. - (85)

____

c) With a swift motion the Nazi officer slapped Mama across her face. (85)

____

3. Imagine that Kirsti had been peeking out of her room and observed what was happening tonight. Because she does not understand what was going on, she might be very confused, or even make up an explanation to satisfy herself. Imagine that when she crawls back into bed , she tries to explain what happened to her doll. Using Kirsti's voice and trying to think the way she would, write that one way conversation.

4. Select a section of this chapter, about one half page in length, where the tension is mounting. Practise it so that you can read it orally and share with your study group, the emotions that you felt. Be prepared to point out to the others specific words or phrases that Lowry used to make you experience this tension.

Chapter 11: Will We See You Again Soon, Peter?

1. Create a short definition for each of these words or phrases, using context clues or a dictionary. Then use the word or phrase in a sentence of your own creation that demonstrates that you understand its meaning.

A)

Word	Meaning
a) distribute (88)	
b) rummaging (88)	
c) refashion (89)	
d) assembled (90)	
e) protruding (91)	
f) gestured (91)	
g) wished ... Godspeed (93)	
h) commotion (93)	

B) **Sentences:**

distribute - ______________________________

____

rummaging - ______________________________

____

refashion - ______________________________

____

assembled - ______________________________

____

protruding - ______________________________

____

gestured - ______________________________

wished... Godspeed - ______________________________

commotion - ______________________________

2. Use your inference skills to figure out what the author is referring to in each of these sentences. Write a one or two sentence explanation for each one.

a) Why is the young mother begging and crying? (90)

b) What could be in the dropper Peter is holding, and why? (90)

c) What does Annemarie mean "to protect one another by not telling". (91)

d) Why does Peter call Mrs. Johansen 'Inge' now? (92)

3. Perhaps the adults who care for you have protected you at some time by not telling you something. What might they have been protecting you from? Ask adults around you until someone tells you a story you can use. Take point form notes to help you remember the story. Be prepared to tell your story orally in your study group, using your notes as reference.

4. Imagine you have been displaced from your home and hustled away in the night the way Ellen and her family have been. You don't know if you will ever see your home or your belongings again. Your family has said you may take one treasure with you, but it must be small enough to fit in your pocket.

a) Take a few moments to decide what you would take, then write a complete descriptive paragraph about it. Remember to describe the object fully, tell the circumstances under which it came into your possession, and tell why it would be the one thing you would choose to save.

or

b) There is one object you would dearly love to take, but it is too big to fit in your pocket. Describe the object fully, tell the circumstances under which it came into your possession, and tell why it would be so hard for you to leave it behind.

Chapter 12: Where Was Mama?

1. When two words are joined together to form a new word, a compound is formed. "Baseball" is an example, and the meaning is a ball game that is played using bases. When a small group of letters is added to the beginning of a word, we say that the word has a prefix. "Unwelcome" is an example, and the prefix "un" changes the meaning so that the word now means "not welcome".

   Sort this group of words into two groups, compound words and words with prefixes. Then write a definition for each words, using the root words to help you.

   a) regained (95)
   b) uneven (95)
   c) unnecessary (95)
   d) upstairs (95)
   e) unfamiliar (97)
   f) oatmeal (97)
   g) somewhere (98)
   h) staircase (99)
   i) overlooked (99)
   j) understood (100)

Compound Word	Root Word with Prefix

a) regained - ______________________________

b) uneven - ______________________________

c) unnecessary - ______________________________

d) upstairs - ______________________________

e) unfamiliar - ______________________________

f) oatmeal - ______________________________

g) somewhere - ______________________________

h) staircase - ______________________________

i) overlooked - ______________________________

j) understand - ______________________________

2. Lois Lowry ends this chapter, as she does many of the other chapters in this book with "cliff-hangers". That means she leaves her readers feeling as though they are hanging on a cliff waiting to find out what happens next.

a) Write an explanation as to why you think an author would do this.

____

b) Find three examples from previous chapters where the cliff-hanger technique has been used. Copy the example, and then create a sentence that a reader might ask in response. Chapter 12 is done for you as an example.

Text: The shape moved. And she knew; it was her mother, lying on the earth.

Reader Response: Oh no! Did the Nazis find them? Is her mother dead?

1. **Text:** ______________________________

Reader Response: ______________________________

2. **Text:** ______________________________

Reader Response: ______________________________

3. **Text:** ______________________________

Reader Response: ______________________________

3. Imagine that **Number the Stars** will be made into a movie, and you have been hired to design the sets. Your designs must be detailed enough so that the set builders can follow them. Use full colour, and labels so that your ideas will be clear to the carpenters, painters, and props people. (Props people are responsible for any objects that need to be on the set, anything from furniture to teapots.) Complete this activity in your sketch book.

a) Create three designs: one for the living room, one for the bedroom, and one for an outside scene from this chapter.

b) When your study group meets, you will imagine that the other members of your group are the carpenters, painters, and props people. Using your designs as a visual reference, explain to these workers how you want the sets to be built.

Chapter 13: Run! As fast As You Can!

1. Find a word or a phrase from the page given that matches each definition.

a) almost fell (101) ______________________________

b) tightened up because it hurt (101) ______________________________

c) fallen and spread out (102) ______________________________

d) someone who consumes too much alcohol (102) ______________________________

e) walked unevenly (102) ______________________________

f) small sticks (103) ______________________________

g) larger than normal (103) ______________________________

h) silly child who is not thinking (105) ______________________________

2. Imagine you are an actor who has been chosen to play the part of either Annemarie or her mother. You are looking over the script now, searching for words or phrases that will help you decide how to act this role. Find five phrases from this chapter that will make your job easier, and tell how you will use them in your work.

Example: "Mama spoke quickly, her voice tense."

If I were playing the part of Mama here I would try to have a tight little voice to show how worried I was, but not scared because I wouldn't want to frighten Annemarie.

1. ______________________________

2. ____________________

3. ____________________

4. ____________________

5. ____________________

3. Imagine you had a magic tape recorder that could record not only what people say, but what they are thinking. Turn the machine on while Annemarie is running along the path toward her uncle, and record what she is thinking. Write down her thoughts.

4. You are going to read this whole chapter aloud as Reader's Theatre. Remember to read only the spoken parts of the text. To help you remember how to do this, look back to chapter 9. You will need one person for Annemarie and one for Mama.

Chapter 14: On The Dark Path

1. For each word given, create a definition using context clues or with help from a dictionary. Then use six of the words in sentences of your own creation that demonstrate your understanding of their meanings.

a) latticed (106) - ____________________

b) populated (108) ____________________

c) snuggle (109) ____________________

d) meadow (109) ____________________

e) churning (110) ____________________

f) segment (110) ____________________

g) overgrown (110) ____________________

h) brusque (110) ____________________

i) lay at anchor (111) ____________________

j) herring (111) ____________________

k) prolong (111) ____________________

l) tantalize (111) ____________________

m) rounded (112) ____________________

n) countless (112) ____________________

o) cautiously (112) ____________________

p) taut (112) ____________________

Sentences:

2. Lois Lowry inserts many aspects into this novel that do not seem to have anything to do with the main theme. There are several examples of fairy tales, of children's stories, and of children playing games of fantasy.

a) Give several examples of these from anywhere in the text.

b) Why do you think the children play these games and tell these stories?

c) Why do you think Ms. Lowry use these stories as part of her novel?

4. This chapter, as many others, is a chapter of contrasts. Choose two paragraphs to read aloud that will demonstrate this. Practise reading them so that you can use your voice to help us hear the contrast. Be ready to tell your study group what it is about these two sections that emphasizes the differences.

Chapter 15: My Dogs Smell Meat!

1. An expression is a group of words used in a not-quite-literal way, but in a way that listeners and readers will understand. When Lois Lowry says "Annemarie's mind raced" we know that she doesn't mean her mind jumped out of her head and competed in the 200 metre dash, but rather that her mind was thinking very quickly. The following are examples of expressions taken from the text. Explain in your own words what they mean.

a) Annemarie **willed herself**, with all her being, to behave as Kirsti would. (113)

b) He noted its brown spots, and **made a face** of disgust. (115)

c) Annemarie **froze**. (116)

d) Then his eyes **locked** on the basket. (116)

2. Our language has many synonyms for lots of words, and sometimes an author's biggest task is choosing just the right one to give the reader a clear picture.

When Lois Lowry describes the dogs as "gulping the bread", she doesn't say "eating" or "chewing" or even "swallowing", although these words would all give approximately the same meaning. When she says "gulping" I can picture those dogs eating that bread in one big bite, and its frightening because they might be going to eat Annemarie that way too.

Find four more examples of places where you feel exactly the right word has been chosen. Explain why you made this choice, as was done in the example.

1. ____

____

____

____

____

____

____

2. ____

____

____

____

____

____

____

3. ____

____

____

____

____

____

4. ____

____

____

____

____

____

3. Divide your page into four. In each section draw the picture that was created in your mind by the examples you chose in question 2. Use the sentence or phrase from the text as a caption for your picture.

1.	2.
3.	4.

4. Find your favourite example from the text of a section where Annemarie sounds like Kirsti. Practise reading it aloud so that when you read it to your study group, you will sound like Kirsti too.

Chapter 16: I Will Tell You Just a Little

1. Using context clues, create a definition for each of the following words or phrases. Check in a dictionary to make sure you are correct. Then use each word or phrase in a sentence of your own creation which demonstrates your understanding of its meaning.

a) warily (120) - ______________________________

b) practised motion (122) - ______________________________

c) on the move (123) - ______________________________

d) drugged (124) - ______________________________

e) concealed (124) - ______________________________

f) confronting (124) - ______________________________

g) udder (124) - ______________________________

h) saw them ashore (126) - ______________________________

i) cramped (127) - ______________________________

Sentences:

a) warily (120) - ______________________________

b) practised motion (122) - ______________________________

c) on the move (123) - ______________________________

d) drugged (124) - ______________________________

e) concealed (124) - ______________________________

f) confronting (124) - ______________________________

g) udder - ______________________________

h) saw them ashore - ______________________________

i) cramped - ______________________________

2. Write a sentence or two to explain what you can infer from the following sections of the story.

a) **Poor Blossom! . . . surprised Blossom didn't kick you.** (120)
Explain what Annemarie had been doing before this chapter began.

____

b) **Mama laughed . . . was on a footstool.** (120)
Explain where Mama has been since the end of the last chapter.

____

c) **He is a very, very brave young man. They all are.**
Explain how Uncle Henrik knows Peter and the others must be brave.

____

d) **. . . often we pile dead fish on the deck as well.**
Explain why the fishermen would do this.

____

e) **If I had not, well—-**
Write what you think the end of his sentence would have been.

____

3. This chapter ends very differently from most of the other chapters in this book.

a) How is it different?

b) Why would Lois Lowry change her style at this point?

4. Find a section in this chapter of about one half page in length that you enjoyed reading. Practise it so that you can read it aloud with confidence to your study group. Tell your group specifically what it was about this section you enjoyed reading.

Chapter 17: All This Long Time

1. Find a word or phrase in the chapter that has the following meaning.

a) patriotic song associated with a group or country (128) ____________________

b) taken care of (128) ____________________

c) someone who talks a lot (129) ____________________

d) crushing, disappointing (129) ____________________

e) empty, sad, lonely (129) ____________________

f) basement (130) ____________________

g) entered without announcement (130) ____________________

h) everything is mixed up (130) ____________________

i) close and open eyes quickly (131) ____________________

j) like a porch, but higher up (131) ____________________

k) plans to be married (131) ____________________

l) become paler (131) ____________________

m) shine (131) ____________________

n) celebrating (132) ____________________

2. Use your skills of inference to explain these situations.

a) Why had Lise not told her parents that she was part of the Resistance movement?

____
____
____
____
____

b) Why did people dust the furniture in other people's apartments?

c) Why had Peter worn a hat at Lise's funeral?

d) Why did Annemarie hide Ellen's necklace in Lise's dress, but not tell her parents?

e) Why is Annemarie going to wear the necklace now, when she never had before?

3. Imagine that **Number the Stars** is being made into a movie. You have been hired as a camera person. Today you are situated on the balcony just behind Annemarie. Draw the scene that you will show the viewers to let them know what Annemarie can see as she looks out. Complete your drawing in your sketch book.

4. In the movie version which we are imagining is being made, the director has decided not to show any visuals during the last chapter. It will be done as a voice over, with scenes of a free Denmark appearing on the screen, sort of like an epilogue. Your study group has been chosen to provided the voices for this section of the movie. You will need someone to play the parts of Annemarie, Papa, and Mama, as well as several narrators to share the narrated portions. Practise your own part so that you can contribute to a smooth and effective production.

Summary Activities

1. Write a letter to Lois Lowry. In it, tell her at least three specific things that you enjoyed about **Number the Stars**. Make sure your letter has an interesting introduction and an appropriate conclusion, and is set up according to standard letter writing format.

2. After receiving so many letters from young people like yourself telling her how much they enjoyed reading this book, Lois Lowry has decided to write a follow-up to it. In chapter 1, Annemarie and Ellen will be reunited when Ellen returns. Ms. Lowry is having trouble getting started, and she has asked you to help her by writing the first three paragraphs for her.

3. Imagine that you have been chosen as casting director for the movie version of **Number the Stars**. It is your job to hire people to play each part. Today you will cast the major roles: Annemarie, Ellen, Mama, Papa, and Kirsti. You may choose an actor that you know of from TV or movies, or you may choose a person whom you know (even yourself if you wish!) to play each character. Explain each choice you make in a short paragraph, being specific in what you say and concentrating on more than just physical characteristics. An example is done for you.

   To play the part of Uncle Henrik, I would choose my friend Eric's father. Uncle Henrik would probably be a quiet man, because he spends most of his day alone fishing, and Eric's dad is very quiet. Even though Eric's dad is very neat and tidy, I think he'd be okay acting in a messy house for a little while. Uncle Henrik is very kind during the scenes with Annemarie, and since Eric's dad is a kindergarten teacher, I think he would be able to show that kindness to children very well.

4. The producer for the movie Number the Stars is hiring the Costume Designer today. Here is the outline of the work portfolio each candidate for the job must submit. You really want this job, so work hard to make your sketches catch the producer's eye.

<u>Requirements</u>:

1. You must submit five full colour sketches.
2. The sketches are to be just of the clothing, not the people wearing it.
3. Each costume is to be for a different character.
4. Any accessories such as shoes or hats are to be included with the sketch.
5. Sketches are to be labelled with the character's name and any other details you wish to include.

5. Imagine you are the host of a radio programme which interviews interesting people. Today you have invited two of the characters from **Number the Stars** to be your guests. It is your job as host to ask interesting questions that will lead the guests to tell stories your listeners will enjoy. Write your script, including both your questions and the characters' answers.

MY SKETCH BOOK

Name: ______________________________

Multiple Choice Questions

Circle the correct answer to complete the sentence.

1. Number the Stars is set in
   a) Denmark
   b) Germany
   c) Canada
   d) Sweden

2. Kirsti wishes she could have
   a) a princess doll with a yellow and pink dress
   b) a yellow dress and pink hair ribbons
   c) a yellow cupcake with pink frosting
   d) a yellow and pink ice cream cone

3. Conditions are difficult for the Danish people because
   a) they have a very mean king
   b) many Danish men are in the army
   c) Danish soldiers are mean to the people
   d) Nazi soldiers are occupying Denmark

4. The holiday that is celebrated during the time of the story is
   a) Christmas
   b) Easter
   c) Hallowe'en
   d) Jewish New Year

5. Soldiers come to the Johansens apartment during the night looking for
   a) Peter
   b) the Rosens
   c) Uncle Henrik
   d) Annemarie

6. The soldiers thought Ellen was not a Johansen because

   a) there were not enough photos in the album
   b) Kirsti told them she wasn't
   c) she was wearing her Star of David necklace
   d) she had dark hair

7. Uncle Henrik lives in

   a) Gilleje
   b) Copenhagen
   c) Germany
   d) Sweden

8. When Mama was a child, she said she had

   a) a dog named Trofast
   b) a grey kitten
   c) a dress like Lise's
   d) a pet deer

9. Uncle Henrik has

   a) a wife named Inge
   b) no brothers or sisters
   c) a boat named Ingeborg
   d) a dog named Trofast

10. God of Thunder is

   a) a Danish children's story by Hans Christian Andersen
   b) the type of gun the Nazi soldiers have
   c) the school play in which Ellen had the starring role
   d) the name Kirsti gave to the kitten

11. Great-aunt Birte is
    a) Annemarie and Kirsti's great aunt
    b) a character in the play Ellen was in
    c) Ellen's great aunt
    d) not a real person

12. According to Uncle Henrik, if you don't know something
    a) you should try to find out
    b) it is easier to be brave
    c) you should not tell anyone
    d) it is easy to find out

13. The mourners didn't bring any food to share because
    a) it was war time and they had no extra food
    b) there was already enough food there
    c) they were not really mourners so there was no need
    d) they didn't know that it was the custom to do that

14. Danish people pay their respects to the dead person by
    a) looking him/her directly in the face
    b) keeping the coffin lid closed
    c) bringing food to put in the coffin
    d) turning out all the lights in the house

15. What is it that Peter reads out loud?
    a) a letter from Ellen's parents
    b) a notice from King Christian
    c) an old testament psalm
    d) a letter Lise wrote to him

16. Ellen's mother says that she is afraid of

    a) going on a boat
    b) German soldiers
    c) the ocean
    d) big dogs

17. Peter gives the baby drugs because

    a) he wants her to go to sleep
    b) she has a fever
    c) he is trying to poison her
    d) the drugs are her vitamins

18. Ellen and her family are taken by boat to

    a) Germany
    b) Sweden
    c) Canada
    d) Denmark

19. Annemarie offers to run to Uncle Henrik because

    a) he has forgotten his lunch
    b) he needs the packet Mr. Rosen dropped
    c) Mama needs him to help with her broken ankle
    d) the cow needs to be milked

20. Mama tells Annemarie that if the soldiers catch her she should pretend to

    a) be Uncle Henrik's daughter
    b) have a broken ankle
    c) be on her way to school
    d) be a silly little girl

Answers to Multiple Choice Questions

1. (a) Denmark
2. (c) a yellow cupcake with pink frosting
3. (d) Nazi soldiers are occupying Denmark
4. (d) Jewish New Year
5. (b) the Rosens
6. (d) she had blond hair
7. (a) Gilleje
8. (a) a dog named Trofast
9. (c) a boat named Ingeborg
10. (d) the name Kirsti gave to the kitten
11. (d) not a real person
12. (b) it is easier to be brave
13. (c) they were not real mourners so there was no need to
14. (a) looking him/her directly in the face
15. (c) an old testament psalm
16. (c) the ocean
17. (a) he wants her to go to sleep
18. (b) Sweden
19. (b) he needs the packet Mr Rosen dropped
20. (d) be a silly little girl

NUMBER THE STARS
BY LOIS LOWRY